Math = Silence

PRAISE FOR *STORYSHARES*

"One of the brightest innovators and game-changers in the education industry."
– Forbes

"Your success in applying research-validated practices to promote literacy serves as a valuable model for other organizations seeking to create evidence-based literacy programs."

- Library of Congress

"We need powerful social and educational innovation, and Storyshares is breaking new ground. The organization addresses critical problems facing our students and teachers. I am excited about the strategies it brings to the collective work of making sure every student has an equal chance in life."
– Teach For America

"Around the world, this is one of the up-and-coming trailblazers changing the landscape of literacy and education."
- International Literacy Association

"It's the perfect idea. There's really nothing like this. I mean wow, this will be a wonderful experience for young people."   - Andrea Davis Pinkney, Executive Director, Scholastic

"Reading for meaning opens opportunities for a lifetime of learning. Providing emerging readers with engaging texts that are designed to offer both challenges and support for each individual will improve their lives for years to come. Storyshares is a wonderful start."
- David Rose, Co-founder of CAST & UDL

Math = Silence

Julian Siminski

STORYSHARES

Story Share, Inc.
New York. Boston. Philadelphia

Published in the United States by Story Share, Inc.

Storyshares
Story Share, Inc.
24 N. Bryn Mawr Avenue #340
Bryn Mawr, PA 19010-3304
www.storyshares.org

Inspiring reading with a new kind of book.

Interest Level: High School
Grade Level Equivalent: 5.7

9781642614718

Book design by Storyshares

Printed in the United States of America

Storyshares Presents

1

Tyler could faintly hear his alarm clock going off under the *Imagine Dragons* song streaming through his ear buds. He rolled over and hit the top of the clock. Then he pulled the covers up over his head and curled up on his side. He did the same thing every weekday morning. It was the only thing about the routine that he liked:

Alarm goes off.

Hit the alarm.

Take out ear buds.

Turn off smartphone.

Roll over for five more minutes.

And then quiet.

Once he got his skinny body out of bed, he would open his window and listen to the songbirds greeting the morning. Then he'd pick up a pad, a piece of artist's charcoal, and begin to sketch.

Last year he decided he would draw what he saw outside his bedroom window every day for a year. He mostly wanted to see if he could do it for 365 days. But also he was curious to see how things changed; the things he didn't usually notice until some big difference occurred.

Tyler was curious overall, much more so than a lot of his classmates. His friend group was small anyway. Mostly because he had been hiding a secret from everyone and he had yet to find the courage to come clean about it. The down side of it was that he spent a lot of time on his own because he just didn't feel like he fit in anywhere.

On the up side, his ability to create was improving every day. Tyler had a knack for figuring out how things worked. He was always coming up with new ideas for inventions that could do things like help the environment. When he was upset about something, he would always fall back on sketching or building something in his dad's wood shop out back.

Tyler's parents knew he was troubled by some unspoken problem. They could tell by how hard he would work on his creative projects. Finding sketches lying about Tyler's room told them he had something on his mind.

They'd explained to Tyler from an early age that the best way to solve a problem is to talk about it. Usually, Tyler took their advice. But then again, he was a boy. And boys in general seemed to struggle to talk about their feelings.

2

As Tyler was pulling his bicycle out of the garage, his best friend, Brody, came riding up.

"Hey, Tyler!"

"Hi, Brody. I thought your mom was driving you to school?"

Brody shrugged his shoulders. "I got up late and she couldn't wait. Did you finish your homework?"

Tyler looked at him for a minute. Then he pulled his homework out of his bag and stuffed it into Brody's. "You know, you might actually learn something if you did it yourself," Tyler said.

"Why? I hate math and I doubt I will ever use it once I finish school."

Tyler shook his head, got on his bike, and the two of them rode towards school.

It was fifth period when Brody rushed into class. He slipped Tyler's homework onto his desk with the skill of a magician. Tyler looked up at Ms. Stoats to make sure she hadn't seen Brody give him back his papers.

"Okay, everyone, listen up!" Ms. Staats said loudly. "Continuing on about how math relates to just about everything, today we are going to talk about Leonardo da Vinci. Da Vinci is considered to be one of the great inventors and mathematicians of the Renaissance."

A young female student raised her hand. Ms. Staats nodded for her to speak. "I thought da Vinci was an artist? Didn't he paint the Mona Lisa?" the student asked.

"That's correct," Ms. Staats answered. "He is considered to be one of the most gifted artists in history."

Ms. Staats tacked a print of the Mona Lisa onto the large cork board at the front of the classroom.

"Was she da Vinci's wife?" one of the students inquired.

"No, but many people have asked the same question," she replied. "This is a reproduction, a copy, of the Mona Lisa. It is one of da Vinci's most famous paintings. But he was also known for many other things. Your job over the next three days is to find what this painting has to do with math. As I said, da Vinci was also a mathematician and an inventor. You have until Friday to come up with your report. We will read some of them aloud in class," Ms. Staats finished.

3

After dinner that night, Tyler opened his laptop and did a Google search for Leonardo da Vinci. He saw a photo of a sketch called the Vitruvian Man. The sketch was of two images of a naked man, one image superimposed on top of the other. One drawing showed the man with his feet together and his arms extended out in a sort of T. In the other image, his legs were apart and his arms extended higher, in a V shape. A circle was drawn around them.

Tyler read on to learn that it was supposed to represent the ideal human proportions. The sketch is often referred to as "The Proportions of Man."

"That's it," Tyler said to himself.

He also found sketches of many of da Vinci's inventions including a drawing for a helicopter, a flying machine, scuba gear, and military inventions like the giant crossbow and the triple barrel canon. Almost all these things were invented in the late 1400s!

The more Tyler read about da Vinci, the more he understood how da Vinci's math abilities played a part in his work. But Tyler also felt connected to da Vinci because he shared so many interests with this long-haired, bearded man from more than 500 years ago.

Then Tyler came across a news story stating that a recently discovered painting of da Vinci's sold in an auction for 450 million dollars! It was a painting of Jesus Christ called, in Italian, "Salvator Mundi," or *Savior of the World*. Tyler wondered what da Vinci would think about his painting selling for so much money. He tried to imagine one of his own sketches being worth that much.

As he looked through the online images of da Vinci's art, he came across one that caught his eye. It was called St. John the Baptist. Tyler was struck by the suggestive pose of the model in the painting. He discovered that the model was an artist named Andrea Salai, a young man thought to be da Vinci's lover.

"Lover?" Tyler said out loud. "Da Vinci was gay? Wow!"

Tyler had never heard that da Vinci was homosexual, and it made him wonder who else was. Suddenly an idea came into his head.

On Friday morning when Tyler's alarm went off, he was already awake, sitting up in bed and typing rapidly on his laptop. He didn't open the window, and he didn't pick up his sketch book. He had a plan; he just wasn't completely sure he could pull it off.

4

While Tyler was walking his bicycle out of the garage, Brody rode up on his mountain bike. "Hey, Tyler!"

Tyler did his best not to make eye contact. "No," is all he said. Brody looked at him, puzzled.

"No? No what?" Brody asked.

"No you can't borrow my homework on da Vinci."

Brody's face screwed up. "Ah man, come on! I promise I will give it back before class!"

Tyler shook his head, got on his bike, and rode away.

As the bell for fifth period rang, Tyler was already sitting at his desk doodling on his smart phone with a drawing app. Brody walked down the aisle and stopped at Tyler's desk with a frown on his face.

"Thanks a lot, bro," Brody said under his breath before walking to his seat. Tyler wanted to explain, but he couldn't - not yet. Besides, Brody really needed to start doing his own homework.

As Ms. Staats started calling on students to read their reports to the class, the stories were mostly what Tyler expected, which was basically copying facts they found on the internet. Tyler was surprised that no one seemed to mention what he discovered, so he finally got up the nerve to raise his hand.

"Okay, Tyler, let's hear what you've got," said Ms. Staats.

5

Tyler got up and nervously made his way to the front of the class.

"Um, I decided to take a different approach with my report. I hope that's alright," he said, throwing a glance in Ms. Staats's direction. She nodded, giving him permission to proceed.

"Leonardo da Vinci was born in 1452 in Vinci, Italy. Basically, his name means Leonardo of Vinci, since that was his town. He was the illegitimate son of Ser Piero da Vinci, a married, prominent businessman, and a local woman who was kind of like a maid."

"Most of us know him as a painter. But he was also famous for being a sculptor, an architect, an engineer, a scientist, and a mathematician. For example, he was known for creating some of the most extensive drawings of the human anatomy—our bones, organs, our muscles, and tendons. That's probably one of the reasons he was such a great artist when it came to drawing people. Like his painting of the Mona Lisa, which is in the Louvre in Paris. If you look at the painting long enough you can see that he really understood proportion. And proportion is math."

Tyler held up his notebook and turned it toward the classroom. "This is the *Vitruvian Man*. It demonstrates da Vinci's knowledge of how our bodies are a mathematical ideal—everything works perfectly when put together."

Tyler stopped, put down his notebook, and cleared his throat. He looked at Ms. Staats and the other students in the class.

"While I was researching online, I also came across a painting of Saint John the Baptist. I was surprised to learn that the model who posed as the saint was also da Vinci's partner in life—his lover—a young man named Salai."

Most of the students listened attentively. But some became uncomfortable with the direction Tyler's report was taking.

"So did his boyfriend pose as the Mona Lisa too?" one boy shouted. Other students began to laugh along.

"No!" Tyler said loudly. "But when I realized that this really, really smart man was gay, I wondered... why I didn't know that before? I wondered how many other famous people in history were also same-sex oriented. I found out that other famous people were gay too, like painter and sculptor Michelangelo and the artists John Singer Sargent and Grant Wood."

"So, big deal," said another boy in the classroom. "Aren't most artists and actors gay anyway, including a lot of the women?"

"That's really dumb," a girl said back to the boy.

Tyler went on. "Alexander the Great and Hadrian, who was one of the emperors of Rome, were also gay. And more recent people like astronaut Sally Ride and people in Congress are lesbian or gay too."

"This is all very interesting," Ms. Staats said, slightly uncomfortable. "But how does this relate back to da Vinci and math?"

6

Tyler shifted from one foot to the other before continuing. "Well, because—because I think these facts should be part of our school curriculum. Like how when we talk about George Washington, we often talk about his wife Martha. Or Obama and Mrs. Obama. Or any number of people covered in our text books..."

Ms. Staats cut him off. "But isn't that personal information? We're not studying relationships here. We're studying history and educational subjects."

Tyler replied quickly. "Isn't education about learning? Well, when I started to research this paper, I didn't know da Vinci was gay. I learned something new. And also, when you look at the Vitruvian Man, the sketch is about all parts equaling the whole. One whole person. It wouldn't be ideal if part of his arm was hidden, would it? So how can gay people be considered part of society if they are hidden from the whole?"

"But why would da Vinci's sexual preference be important to his work?" Ms. Staats asked.

"First of all, it's not a preference," he shot back. "It's an orientation. And secondly, who we are as people dictates a lot about who we are in our life and what we decide to do as a career."

"Bro, why would what some homo does be important to high school?" one of the male students called out.

"Because everyone needs role models. We need to be represented by people who identify the same way we do. Some of us look up to sports figures or our Scout leader. Some of us look to famous rap artists or scientists. But at least in school, there is an unspoken lie that says those role models are heterosexual—straight.

You probably don't think about it if you aren't gay or lesbian or trans or non-conforming. The fact that we never talk about people's orientation, unless they are straight, means there aren't role models for the kids who don't fit into the norm."

"And," Tyler added, "maybe if those kids learned that there were famous, successful people that were just like them, they would feel better about themselves. Maybe it would help them feel like they didn't have to hide their true selves from their friends and family."

"Whoa, bro. Next you're going to say you're gay!" one of the students shouted. He made a limp wrist gesture, which caused many of the students to laugh.

"I am," Tyler said. "I am gay. You still think it's funny?"

The classroom fell silent. Ms. Staats went up to the front of the class. "Okay, I think we can move on now."

"This is important," Tyler insisted. "There are groups of students in different parts of the country who are sponsoring a 'Day of Silence' to bring attention to the fact that we want to be taught about the parts of our history that are left out—the parts that are silenced.

We *all* want to be a part of the whole. There will be a day where students will not speak as a form of protest. I plan to start a group here in our high school that will participate."

Ms. Staats looked at Tyler for a few seconds before she spoke. "I think it's a great idea, Tyler. I don't know how successful you will be here, but I commend you for your bravery."

Many of the students began to applaud Tyler, some even stood up. But some did not. Even so, it was a better reaction than Tyler thought he would get. It brought a small smile to his face.

"Okay, so now we are beginning to see how da Vinci used math to create the proportions of Mona Lisa's face. Any questions about that?" Ms. Staats asked.

7

Riding his bike home, Tyler heard someone shouting behind him. He slowed down and turned to see who it was, expecting trouble from some of the guys at school after revealing his big secret.

"Hey, Tyler, wait up!" Brody shouted.

Tyler stopped until Brody caught up with him. Tyler eyed him nervously.

"Man, I had a feeling you were gay," Brody said.

"Why?" Tyler asked.

"Because whenever we have gym class you always get red in the face and turn away from all the other guys who are getting buck naked in the locker room." He chuckled. "I mean dude, everyone else is looking to see who's got the biggest gun, but not you!"

"Shut up," Tyler said, laughing just a little.

"Don't worry, man." Brody said. "I get a little shy in there too. Do you think that means I'm gay also?"

Tyler finally let out a big laugh and shook his head. "No, Brody. Definitely not."

About The Author

Julian Siminski attended the University of Oxford and is currently the Director of Marketing at LUX ART & Design, an international art consultancy firm specializing in fine art for hospitality, museums, & public spaces. Their creative team has produced content for GUESS, GUESS Kids, Stuart Weitzman, Coca-Cola, Hi-C, Blue Cross of California, and several other companies.

Julian Siminski

About The Publisher

Story Shares is a nonprofit focused on supporting the millions of teens and adults who struggle with reading by creating a new shelf in the library specifically for them. The ever-growing collection features content that is compelling and culturally relevant for teens and adults, yet still readable at a range of lower reading levels.

Story Shares generates content by engaging deeply with writers, bringing together a community to create this new kind of book. With more intriguing and approachable stories to choose from, the teens and adults who have fallen behind are improving their skills and beginning to discover the joy of reading. For more information, visit storyshares.org.

Easy to Read. Hard to Put Down.

Made in the USA
Middletown, DE
21 January 2023

22080188R10021